Jimmy Bolt:
Accidental Supervillain

Written by
Jenny Jinks

Illustrated by
Steven Wood

Chapter 1

Jimmy could not wait to get to school. He looked at his watch: 8:45. If they didn't leave soon they would be late, and he couldn't be late on his first day at Hero High.

"Come on!" Jimmy called to his parents, bouncing up and down on his toes by the front door.

Jimmy Bolt:
Accidental Supervillain

'Jimmy Bolt: Accidental Supervillain'
An original concept by Jenny Jinks
© Jenny Jinks 2021

Illustrated by Steven Wood

Published by MAVERICK ARTS PUBLISHING LTD
Studio 11, City Business Centre, 6 Brighton Road,
Horsham, West Sussex, RH13 5BB
© Maverick Arts Publishing Limited November 2021
+44 (0)1403 256941

A CIP catalogue record for this book is available at the British Library.

ISBN 978-1-84886-845-8

www.maverickbooks.co.uk

This book is rated as: Grey Band (Guided Reading)

"Alright, we're coming," Mum called.

While he was waiting, Jimmy read the letter again for the hundredth time:

Dear Jimmy Bolt,

We are very pleased to offer you a place at Hero High, the most prestigious superhero school in the world. All the greatest superheroes have walked these halls, and soon you will join them to learn your skills and become the very best.

We look forward to welcoming you at 9 am sharp.

Kind regards,

Headmistress Frost

Finally, Mum rushed down the stairs with Dad right behind her, tucking his shirt in.

Jimmy stared at his parents.

"What are you wearing?!" Jimmy cried.

Mum was wearing what looked like a fancy evening dress, and Dad was in a tuxedo!

"Well this is a special occasion. We wanted to look nice for your big day," Mum said, straightening an imaginary wrinkle from her skirt.

"Not everyone gets selected for Hero High, you know." Dad's eyes glistened with pride. Jimmy knew how much this meant to him. Dad hadn't been chosen for Hero High when he was a boy.

And now Jimmy had, Dad was going to make the most of every moment.

Finally they made it into the car.

"You know, I could just run there," Jimmy said, knowing with his super speed he would have got there in half the time.

"And arrive looking all messy and windswept on your first day?" Dad said. "No chance."

Jimmy rolled his eyes, but he didn't argue.

Finally they pulled up outside the huge metal gates of Hero High. It was bang on 9 o'clock, and the caretaker was just closing the gates.

Jimmy dashed out of the car.

"But I wanted to get a photo!" Dad cried.

"Sorry, no time!" Jimmy shouted as he zoomed up to the school and squeezed through the gates just as the caretaker closed them behind him.

Chapter 2

Jimmy loved Hero High. There were so many kids with all sorts of different powers. Jimmy knew that he would have to try extra hard to stand out at a school where everyone was special, and so he was one of the most eager students Hero High had ever seen. He signed up for every club, handed all of his homework in early, and soon he was top of his year.

"So what's on the agenda for today?" Dad asked over breakfast. Dad loved hearing everything there was to know about Hero High.

"We've got super sports first thing," Jimmy grinned. "Then the new mayor is coming in for a special assembly."

Mum and Dad shared a secret look, but nothing got past Jimmy.

"What is it?" Jimmy asked.

"Well," said Dad, pointing at his newspaper, where a huge picture of Mayor March filled the front page. "Rumour has it the new mayor has lots of plans for Sun City. And one of them is a new Super Protection Squad. They might be looking for new recruits from Hero High to join it."

"What?" said Jimmy excitedly. That sounded awesome. Jimmy just *had* to get on that squad!

It was all anyone could talk about when Jimmy got to school. Everyone was buzzing about the Super Protection Squad and who would get picked.

"Everyone knows a hero's job is to save people in trouble," Mayor March announced to the school. "But what if we could stop them getting into trouble in the first place?"

Everyone looked at each other and nodded. It sounded

so simple. Why had nobody thought of it before?

"That's where you come in," Mayor March continued. "I am looking for the best Supers to protect the city and keep everyone out of harm's way. The city needs you!"

The hall erupted with cheers, and everyone rushed to sign up for the new Super Protection Squad. Jimmy was worried. He was only a first year. What if he didn't get chosen?

Luckily he didn't have to wait long to find out. The very next day, a sign was pinned up outside the headmistress's office. A huge crowd gathered round it, as everyone rushed to find out whether they had made the squad or not. Jimmy whizzed over quick as a flash to the front. And finally, right at the bottom of the list, was his name: Jimmy Bolt.

He couldn't believe it—he was on the squad! This was the best day of his life!

Chapter 3

"This is the worst day of my life!" Jimmy moaned.

It was his first day on the Super Protection Squad. Jimmy had been imagining all the scary and exciting jobs they might get to do—like scaling tall buildings and catching bad guys.

But when Mayor March explained what they would actually be doing, he wasn't so excited any more.

"Welcome, new recruits!" Mayor March smiled at the Super Protection Squad. "I have brought in some new rules recently. Your job is to patrol Sun City and make sure everyone is following them."

Jimmy looked down at the list in his hand.

• Look both ways before crossing the road.

• No climbing trees.

• Do not eat before swimming.

• No littering, especially banana peels.

The list went on and on.

"Any rule breakers will be given a fine. Now go out there and make Sun City safe!"

The squad had been walking the streets for hours now, and they had given out three fines and one set of directions. This was not what Jimmy had imagined being a superhero would be like. He didn't feel super at all, except maybe super bored.

But Mayor March wasn't done yet.

"Things are worse than I thought," Mayor March said as they patrolled round the park. He'd joined them after he finished his work. "Look how steep that slide is. Look how high that child is swinging. No safety harness? No landing mats? It's just asking for trouble. From now on, the park is officially off limits. It is much too dangerous!"

"What?" Jimmy asked. Was he serious? "But everybody loves the park. And there's hardly ever any accidents."

"Hardly ever? That isn't good enough! I want Sun City to be the safest place on the planet!" Mayor March roared.

"Now get those people out of there. NOW!"

Jimmy and his classmate, Astro, looked at each other. Astro shrugged and started sending the children home. But Jimmy couldn't believe it. It was completely ridiculous. And Mayor March was only just getting started. New rules went up every day:

- No running.

- No going out after dark.

- No junk food.

The mayor was banning anything fun. And all in the name of safety.

"Can you believe this?" Jimmy asked Astro at lunch one day. "What's he going to ban next, laughing?"

"He did that first thing this morning," Astro said matter-of-factly. "In case people choke or strain a muscle."

Jimmy's jaw dropped. He hoped Astro was joking, but he looked deadly serious.

"We aren't going to follow his orders, are we? They're ridiculous!"

Astro shrugged. "Our job is to keep people safe. And you have to admit; Sun City has been much quieter since the Super Protection Squad started. I think Mayor March is doing a pretty good job."

Jimmy couldn't believe it. Was he the only one who thought the mayor had gone too far? Mayor March was squeezing all the fun out of Sun City, and there was no way that Jimmy was going to play any part in it.

Chapter 4

"Quick! Let's go," Jimmy whispered. A group of children followed him as they crept towards the park. "I'll stand watch. You go and play."

The children laughed as they ran onto the playground. Jimmy smiled. This was how it should be. And anyone who thought otherwise must be crazy.

"What are you doing?" Astro asked Jimmy, as he and some members of the Super Protection Squad patrolled past.

"What's the harm in children having fun?" Jimmy asked.

"It's against the rules," Astro said.

"The rules are ridiculous," Jimmy said. "Nobody is getting hurt."

"Well..." Astro said.

And then they heard a loud cry. Jimmy and Astro raced to the park. A child was lying on the floor, crying. He had tripped over a tuft of grass and grazed his knee.

"Look what you've done," Astro said to Jimmy. "I'm going to have to report this."

"That could have happened anywhere! He just tripped on some grass!"

"Hmmm, you're right," Astro said.

Thank goodness, thought Jimmy. Finally Astro was seeing sense.

"All grass should be off limits. I should suggest that to Mayor March."

Before Jimmy could say anything, Astro was already walking away, making notes in his notebook.

"Deliberately going against my orders? Getting children hurt? What were you thinking?" Mayor March shouted.

Jimmy stared at his feet. He couldn't believe Astro had told on him.

"This sort of behaviour will not be tolerated. I expect the city's heroes to set a good example and follow the rules, not be the ones breaking them. I'm sorry to have to do this, but you are off the squad!"

"What?" Jimmy cried.

"The city will be safer without you. Hand over your badge."

Jimmy ripped the Super Squad badge from his suit and stormed away. The squad was stupid anyway. He was better off without it. If only he could get everyone else to see that too, then everything could go back to normal.

But try as he might to convince everyone at school that Mayor March was stark raving mad, nobody would listen. Astro wasn't even talking to him anymore. Whenever he saw Jimmy coming, he and his friends turned and walked the other way.

"Astro, wait," Jimmy called after him. "Don't worry, I'm not mad at you for getting me kicked off the squad."

Astro spun around.

"Mad at me?" he spat. "I should be mad at you! Your reckless behaviour nearly got me thrown out too!"

"Reckless behaviour?" Jimmy was shouting now. "You're starting to sound just like the mayor! We have to stop this, before Mayor March gets completely out of control!"

"JIMMY BOLT!"

Jimmy froze. The corridor had gone suddenly very cold. Slowly he turned around to see Headmistress Frost and Mayor March walking towards him. Mayor March had a horrible smirk on his face.

"How dare you speak about your mayor like that," the headmistress said. "I am very disappointed in you. Hero High expects better from its students. Being here is a privilege. One that I am not sure that you deserve."

"No, Headmistress please..." Jimmy said.

"I am sorry, but you have left me with no choice. I am afraid, Jimmy Bolt, that you are expelled from Hero High."

Chapter 5

Jimmy's whole world was falling apart. Just moments ago he had everything he ever wanted: he was top of his year at Hero High, with a place on the Super Squad. Everything was perfect. And now it was all gone.

Jimmy didn't know what to do or where to go. He couldn't go home; his parents would be so disappointed. So he wandered the streets. There was already a barrier up around the local green. Jimmy couldn't believe Mayor March really had banned walking on grass.

The sun was starting to go down. It was against the rules to be out after dark. If Jimmy got caught he would be in big trouble. Again. He had to stay out of the way.

Jimmy spotted a couple of Super Squad members further along the street. He ducked down a dark alley just in time and waited. Jimmy couldn't believe he was hiding from people who used to be his friends. Finally the Super Squad moved on, and Jimmy breathed a sigh of relief.

"What are you doing here? You're one of them," came a voice from the darkness, making Jimmy jump. "Shouldn't you be off arresting people?"

Jimmy laughed bitterly. "Not anymore. I just got kicked out of the Super Squad. *And* the academy. All because of stupid Mayor March." Jimmy didn't even know why he said that, it just came out. He didn't even know who he was talking to, but he had a weird feeling he could trust them.

"Really?" Another voice said, and two people stepped out of the shadows. They were just kids, about the same age as Jimmy.

"Who are you?" Jimmy asked.

"I'm Winnie," said the girl, although Jimmy was sure her mouth didn't actually move when she spoke. "And this is Vex."

When Jimmy looked at Vex he felt a strange feeling of calm come over him. He liked these two already, though he wasn't quite sure why.

"We have powers, just like you." said Vex, "Except we weren't allowed into Hero High. Instead, we were put on the Supervillain List. We're on the run."

"But why?" Jimmy asked. He started to feel a bit uneasy at the thought of being stuck in a dark alley with two supervillains. But almost as soon as he felt it he began to feel oddly calm again. Something very strange was going on.

"Don't worry, we aren't dangerous." Vex said. "The mayor decided that our powers were too dark to be heroes. He didn't even give us a chance!"

Jimmy began to bubble with anger. This was too much, even for Mayor March.

"That's it, I've had enough of Mayor March. He thinks he can do whatever he wants. It's about time somebody stopped him, once and for all," Jimmy said. "There is a very good chance we might end up in some serious trouble, so if you don't want to be involved I understand."

Winnie and Vex looked at each other and smiled.

"We're in!"

Chapter 6

Jimmy, Winnie and Vex crept through Jimmy's front door. His dad was asleep at the dining room table, a cup of coffee still in his hand.

The sound of the door woke him up.

"Jimmy, where have you been? I've been so worried," Dad said. "Who are these people? What are you doing with them?" Dad looked panicked.

"Don't worry, we're friends," Vex said, and Jimmy noticed Dad instantly relax. Could Vex control people's emotions? That was so cool! He would have to remember to ask him about that later. But for now it would have to wait.

"Dad, I need to explain," Jimmy said.

"There's no time," Dad said. "You can't stay here. You've been put on the list. They're coming for you."

"What list?" Jimmy asked. "Who's coming?"

Dad handed Jimmy a letter. Jimmy had a bad feeling as he began to read:

Dear Mr and Mrs Bolt,

Your son, Jimmy Bolt, has officially been placed on the Supervillain List. Being a supervillain is against the rules. Please ensure your son hands himself in, or the Super Protection Squad will be sent to collect him.

Signed,

Mayor March

Jimmy was a supervillain now? How could this have happened?!

"I can't believe this!" Jimmy cried.

"What are you going to do?" Dad asked. "The Super Squad will be here any minute."

Jimmy was thinking fast. Nowhere was safe, not now the Super Squad was after him.

"I've got to get away from Sun City, and fast," Jimmy said.

Jimmy and Dad looked at each other.

"Then there's only one place you can go," Dad said.

Jimmy nodded, gave his dad a quick hug, grabbed Winnie and Vex, and zoomed away.

Chapter 7

"Where are we going?" Winnie asked. They hadn't stopped running since they left Jimmy's house, and now they were on a train heading out of Sun City.

"Why are we running away? I thought we were going to fight?" Vex said.

"We *are* going to fight," Jimmy said. "But if we're going to take down Mayor March once and for all, we are going to need some serious super backup."

Jimmy had always hoped he would be part of an epic battle between superheroes and supervillains. He just never thought *he* would be the supervillain! But the three of them would never be able to bring down the mayor on their own, especially with his Super Squad to protect him. And there was only one person Jimmy knew that was strong enough, brave enough and reckless enough to help them.

Finally the train stopped in the middle of the countryside, and the three got off.

They walked up to a big farmhouse.

"What are we doing *here?*" Vex said.

"Trust me," said Jimmy, and he knocked on the door.

An elderly man answered.

"Hello?" he said, peering out.

Vex and Winnie gasped.

"Oh my goodness, you're... you're..." Vex said.

"Jet! The most amazing superhero Sun City has ever seen!" Winnie said.

"Hi Grandad," Jimmy grinned.

"Fancy seeing you here, Jimmy. You'd better come in."

They all sat round Grandad's kitchen table as he shooed a chicken out the back door.

"I don't think you've come all the way out here for some fun on the farm. So, who wants to tell me what's been going on?" Grandad asked.

So Jimmy, Winnie and Vex explained everything that had happened since Mayor March got into power.

"Well, goodness me, what a pickle. But I don't know how you think I can help," Grandad said.

"You're the strongest, toughest, most powerful superhero that ever lived!" Winnie said.

"Ex-superhero," Grandad corrected her, turning to stare out the window. "I'm retired now, you know. I just want a quiet life. I've had enough of all that excitement."

"I can make him want to do it if you like," Vex whispered to Jimmy. But Jimmy shook his head. He had spotted the twinkle in Grandad's eye when they had started talking about taking down the mayor. He knew Grandad missed it all really. He just needed a little push.

"Come on, Grandad. Come out of retirement for this one last job. Your city needs you."

That did the trick. When Grandad turned round he had a smile on his face and a glint in his eye.

"Well, perhaps I could dust off the old suit and see if it still fits!" Grandad said.

"Yes!" said Jimmy, Vex and Winnie together.

Chapter 8

With Jet on their side, Jimmy knew there was no way they could fail.

They stormed back to Sun City (with the help of Grandad Jet's jet stream, which whizzed them there on a gust of wind faster than a speeding train) and straight up to Mayor March's mansion.

They hammered on the door.

"No hammering on doors, it's against the rules," came a voice from behind the door.

"I'll show him what I think of his rules," Grandad said, and blew down the door like it was made of paper.

"Hey! What do you think you are doing?" Mayor March

yelled. "That could have taken someone's eye out!" Then he saw Jet, and his eyes widened. "Jet? Is it... is it really you? I thought you had left Sun City."

"I will never leave Sun City as long as the people need me to protect them from people like you," Jet said. "You need to stop all this safety nonsense."

"Safety isn't nonsense! These people should be thanking me! I'm the only one trying to keep them safe!" Mayor March began gabbling, and Jimmy knew that Vex was working

his powers on the mayor, just as they had planned. "When I was just a boy I climbed a tree and got stuck. I waited for ages for a superhero to come to my rescue. Nobody ever came. In the end, I jumped and I broke my arm. If the Super Squad had been around then, none of that would ever have happened. But the heroes didn't care about me. Nobody did. I want to stop anyone else from suffering like I did. Am I the only one who cares about their lives?"

"But you aren't letting them live!" Jimmy cried. "Nobody can do *anything* anymore because of your rules. They might as well be locked up."

"Well, maybe that's for the best!" Mayor March said, going very red in the face. "If they can't handle my rules, maybe they *should* all be locked up. Then they will learn!"

Jimmy couldn't believe what he was hearing. And neither could the people of Sun City. Because while Mayor March was saying all of this, Winnie had been using her superpower—the power to transmit thoughts from one person to another—to let the whole of Sun City hear everything that the mayor was saying. Now everyone knew the truth about how dangerous the mayor really was.

Soon a huge crowd had gathered around Mayor March's mansion, and they were not happy.

Chapter 9

Mayor March looked out of the window. He knew he had been beaten, but he was not going down without a fight. He turned to Jet.

"Join me. Lead my Super Squad. Arrest these supervillains, or I shall arrest you too, and place you on the Supervillain List along with your rule-breaking rebellious grandson."

Oh no, thought Jimmy. He knew how much Grandad's reputation meant to him. Being a superhero had been his whole life. He couldn't let Mayor March take that away from him.

But Jet just smiled. "I will never join you," Jet laughed.

"And if that makes me a supervillain then so be it!"

Yes! thought Jimmy. *Go Grandad!*

Suddenly, the room felt very cold, and Headmistress Frost burst through the doors, along with the Super Squad. They gasped when they saw Jet.

"Super Squad, arrest these villains. Lock them up. They have broken all of my rules," the mayor cried.

"Sorry," said Astro. "But we are not here for them. We are here for you."

And as quick as a flash, the Super Squad swarmed in and had Mayor March in handcuffs.

"We heard everything you said," said Headmistress Frost. "And nobody has the right to take away the freedom of the people of Sun City."

"But..." cried Mayor March as he was dragged away, kicking and screaming. "I don't understand. I was just trying to keep you safe! You don't know what you are doing!"

Chapter 10

Headmistress Frost walked over to Jimmy. Jimmy stared at his feet. He had a horrible feeling he was about to get into even more trouble. But then Jet stepped forward.

"I have a few things I need to say to you," Jet said to Headmistress Frost, puffing himself up as tall as he could. He looked very grand, standing there in his suit (even if it was a little snug around the edges these days). Headmistress Frost took half a step backwards. "My grandson should never have been kicked out of your academy. All Jimmy and his friends have done is look out for the people of this city when nobody else would. Even at the risk of getting themselves in trouble. I insist that they are removed from the Supervillain List immediately and allowed straight back to into your academy with a full pardon! These fine young heroes are a shining example of what being a hero is all about, and you should consider yourself lucky to have them in your school."

Headmistress Frost gulped. "I completely agree," she said.

Jimmy looked up in shock. He had not been expecting that.

"You have shown courage, strength, and intelligence today. I am sorry that I didn't see what Mayor March was really doing. Without your bravery, who knows how far he might have gone. And I see we have two new heroes here." She turned to Vex and Winnie, who both blushed. "Your powers seem quite remarkable, just the sort of thing we need on our side. We look forward to welcoming you to Hero High."

"I didn't even make her say that!" Vex whispered, grinning from ear to ear.

"Come on, come on!" cried Jimmy as he waited by the front door.

"Alright, I'm coming!" Grandad said, running down the stairs.

They jumped in the car and Dad drove them to Hero High. They pulled up outside the huge metal gates at bang on 9 o'clock. Jimmy looked up at the huge building. Suddenly he felt nervous. What if nobody wanted him back? He had been a supervillain, after all, even if it was only for a day.

Don't worry, you'll be fine, a voice popped up in his head, and then he felt a warm, calm feeling spread over him. Jimmy turned around, and there were his friends walking towards him, huge smiles on their faces.

"I'm going to have to get used to you both doing that," Jimmy laughed. "Ready?"

"Yeah!" Vex and Winnie cried.

"I suppose," Grandad said. "What if they don't like me?"

"I can help with that, if you want me to?" Vex said.

"Thanks," Grandad chuckled. "I'll let you know."

Grandad adjusted his newly fitted super suit.

"You'll be great, Grandad," Jimmy said, giving him a quick hug.

"It's Professor Jet now, thank you," Grandad smiled. "How do I look?"

Jimmy looked up at his Grandad and smiled. "You look super!" he said.

Discussion Points

1. Who is behind all the new rules in Sun City?

2. What happens when Jimmy lets children play in the playground?

a) Jimmy falls off a swing

b) Mayor March catches them

c) One child hurts themselves

3. What was your favourite part of the story?

4. How do Jimmy, Winnie and Vex stop the mayor?

5. Why do you think Winnie and Vex were put on the Supervillain List?

6. Who was your favourite character and why?

7. There were moments in the story when Jimmy had to **think outside the box**. Where do you think the story shows this most?

8. What do you think happens after the end of the story?

Book Bands for Guided Reading

The Institute of Education book banding system is a scale of colours that reflects the various levels of reading difficulty. The bands are assigned by taking into account the content, the language style, the layout and phonics. Word, phrase and sentence level work is also taken into consideration.

The Maverick Readers Scheme is a bright, attractive range of books covering the pink to grey bands. All of these books have been book banded for guided reading to the industry standard and edited by a leading educational consultant.

To view the whole Maverick Readers scheme, visit our website at

www.maverickearlyreaders.com

Or scan the QR code to view our scheme instantly!

Pink
Red
Yellow
Blue
Green
Orange
Turquoise
Purple
Gold
White
Lime
Brown
Grey

Maverick Chapter Readers
(From Lime to Grey Band)